characters created by lauren child

Boo! MADE you juMp!

Grosset & Dunlap

Charlie
and
Lola™

Text based on the script written by Dave Ingham

Illustrations from the TV animation

produced by Tiger Aspect

GROSSET & DUNLAP
Published by the Penguin Group
Penguin Group (USA) Inc., 375 Hudson Street, New York, New York 10014, USA
Penguin Group (Canada), 90 Eglinton Avenue East, Suite 700, Toronto, Ontario M4P 2Y3, Canada
(a division of Pearson Penguin Canada Inc.)
Penguin Books Ltd., 80 Strand, London WC2R 0RL, England
Penguin Group Ireland, 25 St. Stephen's Green, Dublin 2, Ireland
(a division of Penguin Books Ltd.)
Penguin Group (Australia), 250 Camberwell Road, Camberwell, Victoria 3124, Australia
(a division of Pearson Australia Group Pty. Ltd.)
Penguin Books India Pvt. Ltd., 11 Community Centre, Panchsheel Park, New Delhi—110 017, India
Penguin Group (NZ), 67 Apollo Drive, Rosedale, North Shore 0745, Auckland, New Zealand
(a division of Pearson New Zealand Ltd.)
Penguin Books (South Africa) (Pty.) Ltd., 24 Sturdee Avenue,
Rosebank, Johannesburg 2196, South Africa

Penguin Books Ltd., Registered Offices: 80 Strand, London WC2R 0RL, England

3 1350 00317 8672

Library of Congress Control Number: 2006100774

ISBN 978-0-448-44696-7   10 9 8 7 6 5

I have this little sister, Lola.
She is small and very funny.
I am always making her jump . . .

But she can

NEVER

make me jump.

So Lola says,
"But I really want to
make you jump, Charlie."

And I say,
"Okay, Lola, but that
will **NEVER** happen."

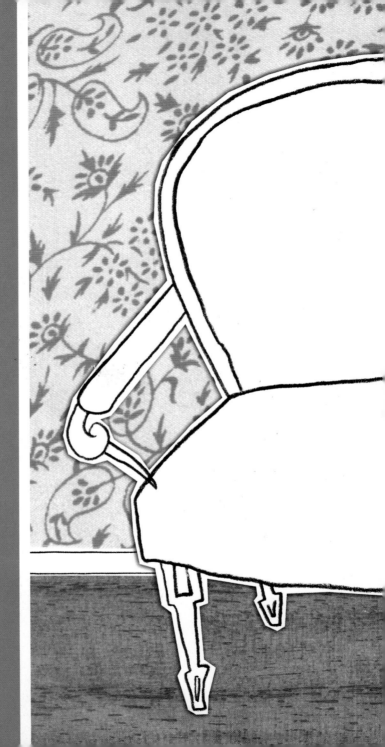

In the park,
    Lola and Lotta scream,

"Boo!"

Lola says,
"You jumped, Charlie.
    I saw you."

And I say,
    "Don't be silly, Lola.
You'll never
    make ME jump."

Later, Lola and Lotta
try to **scare** me and
Marv while we watch TV.

"Oooooohhh..."

"Ooooooohhhh..."

So I say,
    "Hi, Lola."
And Marv says,
    "Hi, Lotta."

That night Lola says,

"I'm going to tell you
a really **scary**
story about a terribly,
terrible very old castle
full of **icky** sticky spiders."

So I say,
"Oh, this story won't
make anyone **jump**."

But Lola says,
"Yes it WILL, Charlie."

"Once upon a time,
 there were two boys
and two not quite so
       biggish small girls.
And they were lost.

They were SO lost
that they went up to a
     Spooky castle
to ask the way."

"They opened the door
of the **scary** castle and
went up the **creaky** stairs."

Then Lotta asks,
"Do we have to go up there?"

"Yes," says Lola.
"That's what you do in
scary stories . . .

And, as they followed
the biggest boy up the
creaky stairs, they heard—"

"A **ghost!**" shouts Marv.

"I'm scared," says Lotta.
"I'm **NOT**," I say.

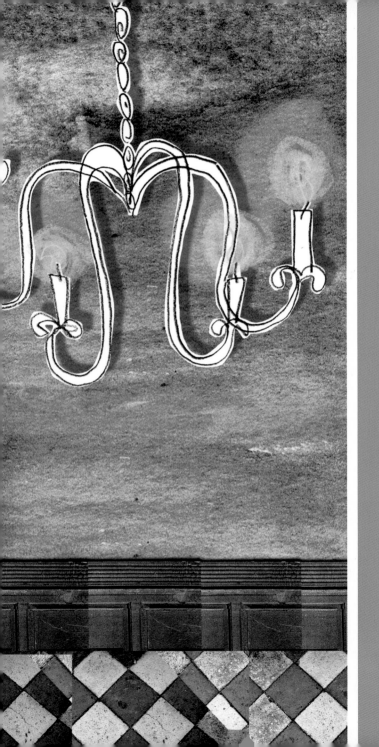

"Anyway, at the very very top of the stairs," says Lola, "there was another great **big** ENORMOUS door.

And as the boy, who looked a bit like Charlie, turned the handle, the ghosty sound got louder and LOUDER...

And do you know who it was?" asks Lola.

Meow

"It was Twinkle!
      Mrs. Elmore's kitten
from next door."

"Oh, Lola!" I say.

"How is a little furry
    animal going to make
anyone **jump**?"

But just then . . .

"AHHHHH!"

I shout.

"SIZZLES, you really made me **jump**."

"Hmmm," says Lola.

"Now I know how to make you **jump**, Charlie."

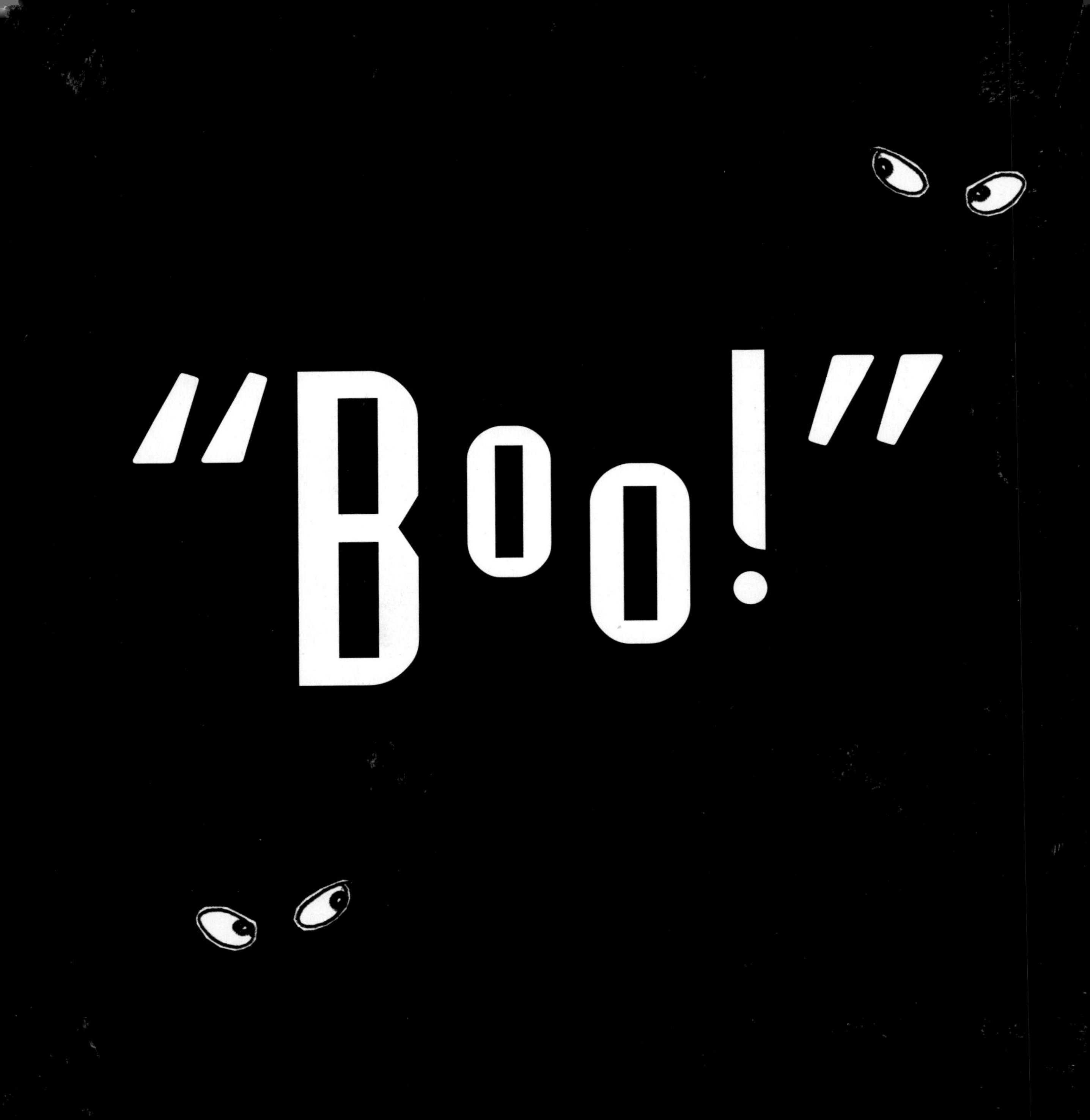
"Boo!"